TEDD ARNOLD

HUGGLY'S ®
BIG MESS

SCHOLASTIC INC.

Cartwheel
B·O·O·K·S·®

New York   Toronto   London   Auckland   Sydney
Mexico City   New Delhi   Hong Kong

For Teddy,
Sam, Wesley,
Andrew, Linda,
and Lindsey
— T. A.

ISBN 0-439-13501-X
Copyright © 2001 by Tedd Arnold.
All rights reserved. Published by Scholastic Inc.
HUGGLY and THE MONSTER UNDER THE BED are trademarks and/or registered trademarks of Tedd Arnold.
SCHOLASTIC, CARTWHEEL BOOKS, and associated logos are trademarks and/or registered trademarks of Scholastic Inc.

Library of Congress Cataloging-in-Publication Data available.

12 11 10 9 8 7 6 5 4 3 2 1   01 02 03 04 05 06

Printed in the U.S.A.
First printing, September 2001

Huggly burst into the Secret Slime Pit. "Hey Booter! Grubble! See what I made?"

"What is it?" asked Booter.

"What's that funny smell?" asked Grubble.

"It's pizza," said Huggly. "Remember the time we crawled up from under the people child's bed and explored the people world until we found pizza? Well, I decided to go up there and make it myself!"

"I don't know," said Booter. "It looks different."

"And it smells different," added Grubble.

"Well," said Huggly, "you know the rule — monsters aren't supposed to take people stuff unless it's been thrown away. So I could only use what was in the trash can." He set his pizza down.

"See? These are old tomato skins and potato peels. These are dead flies. Look at these cool bottle caps. And this cheese has fuzzy, green spots."

"Anything from the people world sounds better than these dried cave worms and rock chips," said Grubble. "Let's eat!"

Booter noticed Huggly's dirty hands and tail. "Making pizza looks like messy work," she said. "I hope you cleaned up after yourself. That's another rule. Put people stuff back the way you found it."

"Oops!" said Huggly. "I forgot."

"You better go clean up your mess," said Grubble. "I'll watch this pizza till you get back."

"You're right," sighed Huggly. "I'd better do it right now. The people will be waking up soon."

Huggly hurried through the tunnel, back to the hatchway that opened
beneath the people child's bed. He peeked out from under the bed.
"Whew, I'm lucky!" he whispered to himself. "Everything is still quiet."

Silently, Huggly slipped out of the people child's room. He tip-toed down the stairs and made his way to the people food room.

"Oops! I guess I left the light on, too," Huggly muttered. He looked around at the mess he had made and groaned, "I have a lot to do."

Huggly went to work.

He mopped up spills,
wiped off smudges, and
swept the floor.

Then he stopped,
looked around, and
scratched his head.
"I don't remember where
any of this stuff belongs."

Finally, all that remained was a pile of rubbish. Huggly scooped it up. But with his arms full, he couldn't see where he was going. Suddenly he stepped on something slippery and tumbled headfirst into the trash can.

Huggly tried to yell, "Help! I'm stuck!" but the trash can muffled his voice and it sounded like, "Hep! Um tuck!"

He kicked his feet. The trash can wiggled. He kicked his feet and swished his tail. The trash can wobbled. He kicked his feet, swished his tail, and hollered, "Hep! Um tu-u-u-uck!" The trash can fell over.

Huggly struggled to his feet, but he couldn't get the trash can off his head. He staggered to where he thought the kitchen door was. *Bump!* He bounced backward.

Huggly stumbled in a different direction. *Bump!* He bounced back again.

Huggly tripped and sat down in something. It was an aquarium! The people child's pet turtle bit Huggly's tail and held on. Huggly didn't know where he was going. He just got up and ran! The turtle held on.

Somehow Huggly made it through the kitchen door, but —*CLANG!*— he bumped into a metal contraption. The people child's pet bird woke up and screeched.

The bird chased Huggly. Huggly kept running. The turtle held on.

Huggly zigged and zagged until—*WHUMP!*—he ran into something soft. The people child's pet cat woke up and hissed.

The cat chased the bird. The bird chased Huggly. Huggly kept running. The turtle held on.

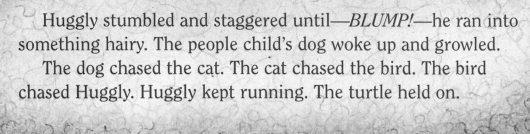

Huggly stumbled and staggered until—*BLUMP!*—he ran into
something hairy. The people child's dog woke up and growled.
The dog chased the cat. The cat chased the bird. The bird
chased Huggly. Huggly kept running. The turtle held on.

Huggly finally found the stairs. He scrambled
to the top and hurried down the hallway.

Huggly ran through the first doorway until—*BLAP!*—he ran into something warm. The people child's little sister woke up and screamed.

The little sister chased the dog. The dog chased the cat. The cat chased the bird. The bird chased Huggly. Huggly kept running. The turtle held on.

Huggly ran blindly into the next bedroom until—*FLUMP!*—he ran into something big. The people child's parents woke up with a start and hollered, "What!?!"

The people parents chased the little sister. The little sister chased the dog. The dog chased the cat. The cat chased the bird. The bird chased Huggly. Huggly kept running. The turtle held on.

Just then, in the bedroom across the hall, Booter and Grubble peeked out from under the people child's bed.

"Huggly's been gone a long time," Grubble whispered.

"Yeah," said Booter. "That mess he made must have been huge. Let's go help him clean up."

Booter and Grubble tiptoed to the door. Suddenly they saw a crowd of creatures and people charging right at them. The first creature ran—*SMACK!*—into them and they tumbled backward.

"Hep! Um tuck!" Huggly yelled.

"Is that you, Huggly?" cried Grubble.

Booter and Grubble yanked the trash can off Huggly's head. At that moment, the people mother, the people father, the little sister, the dog, the cat, and the bird ran into them and they all fell on top of one another. In the confusion, the three monster friends slipped under the bed.

The people child woke up. His whole family and his pets were with him. Trash was everywhere. "Who made this mess?" he asked, rubbing his sleepy eyes.

His father and mother looked at the little sister. The little sister looked at the dog. The dog looked at the cat. The cat looked at the bird. The bird looked for Huggly, but he was gone.

"We'll talk about it in the morning," said the mother, and they all went back to bed.

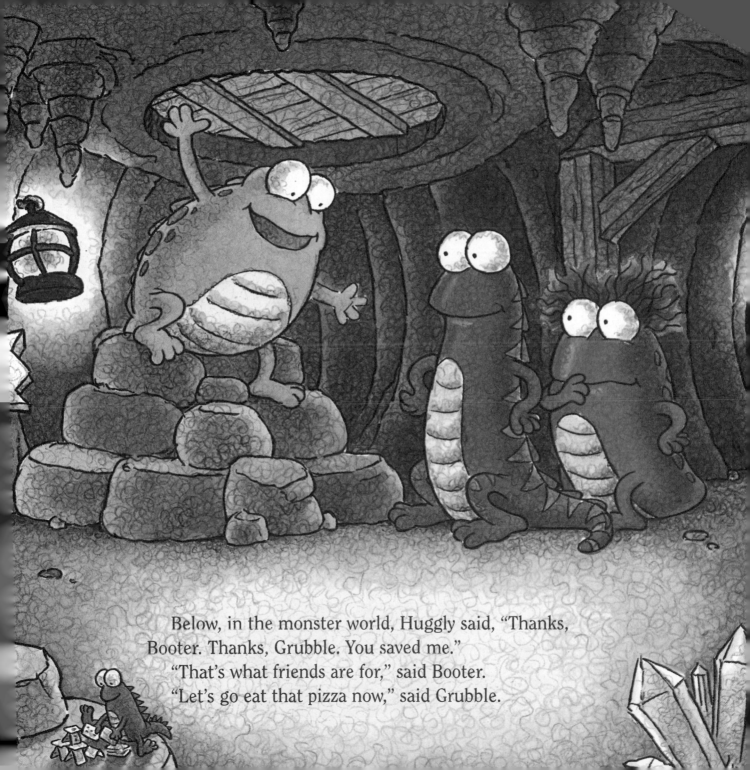

Below, in the monster world, Huggly said, "Thanks, Booter. Thanks, Grubble. You saved me."

"That's what friends are for," said Booter.

"Let's go eat that pizza now," said Grubble.

"Ouch!" said Huggly. He looked at his tail. The turtle was still holding on. He plucked the little creature off and carefully reached up to return it to the people world. Then Huggly joined his friends for some delicious pizza back at the Secret Slime Pit.